33.66

T0153550

OXFORD COUNTY LIBRARY

WOODINGFORD LODGE
RECREATION &
VOLUNTEER SERVICES

LITTLE,
BROWN

1837

LARGE
PRINT

OXFORD COUNTY LIBRARY

Also by James Patterson

The Thomas Berryman Number
Season of the Machete
See How They Run
The Midnight Club
Along Came a Spider
Kiss the Girls
Hide & Seek
Jack & Jill
Miracle on the 17th Green (with Peter de Jonge)
Cat & Mouse
When the Wind Blows
Pop Goes the Weasel
Black Friday
Cradle and All
Roses Are Red
1st to Die
Suzanne's Diary for Nicholas
Violets Are Blue
2nd Chance (with Andrew Gross)
The Beach House (with Peter de Jonge)
Four Blind Mice
The Jester (with Andrew Gross)
The Lake House

The Big Bad Wolf

OXFORD COUNTY LIBRARY

A NOVEL BY

JAMES PATTERSON

LITTLE, BROWN AND COMPANY

LARGE PRINT

Copyright © 2003 by James Patterson

All rights reserved. No part of this book may be repro-
duced in any form or by any electronic or mechanical
means, including information storage and retrieval
systems, without permission in writing from the
publisher, except by a reviewer who may quote brief
passages in a review.

First Large Print Edition

The Large Print Edition published in accord with the
standards of the N.A.V.H.

The characters and events in this book are fictitious.
Any similarity to real persons, living or dead, is
coincidental and not intended by the author.

Library of Congress Cataloging-in-Publication Data
Patterson, James.
        The big bad wolf : a novel / by James
Patterson — 1st ed.
            p. cm.
        ISBN 0-316-74384-4
        1. Cross, Alex (Fictitious character) — Fiction.
    2. African American psychologists — Fiction.
    3. Government investigators — Fiction. 4. Forensic
    psychology Fiction. 5. Washington (D.C.) —
    Fiction. 6. Slave trade — Fiction. 7. Kidnapping —
    Fiction. I. Title.
    PS3566.A822B54 2003
    813'.54 — dc21

                                        2003056196

10   9   8   7   6   5   4   3   2   1

Q-FF

Printed in the United States of America

For Joe Denyeau

Prologue

THE GODFATHERS

THERE WAS an improbable murder story told about the Wolf that had made its way into police lore and then spread quickly from Washington to New York to London and to Moscow. No one knew if it was actually the Wolf. But it was never officially disproved, and it was consistent with other outrageous incidents in the Russian gangster's life.

According to the story, the Wolf had gone to the high-security supermax prison in Florence, Colorado, on a Sunday night in early summer. He had bought his way inside to meet with the Italian mobster and don Augustino "Little Gus" Palumbo. Prior to this visit, the Wolf had a reputation for being impulsive and sometimes lacking patience. Even so, he had been planning this meeting with Little Gus Palumbo for nearly two years.

He and Palumbo met in the Security Housing Unit of the prison, where the New York gangster had been incarcerated for seven years. The purpose of the meeting was to reach an arrangement to unite the East Coast's Palumbo family with the Red Mafiya, thereby forming one of the most powerful and ruthless crime syndicates in the world. Nothing like it had ever been attempted. Palumbo was said to be skeptical, but he agreed to the meeting just to see if the Russian could get inside Florence prison — and then manage to get out again.

From the moment they met, the Russian was respectful of the sixty-six-year-old don. He bowed his head slightly as they shook hands and almost appeared shy, contrary to his reputation.

"There's to be no physical contact," the captain of the guards said from the intercom into the room. His name was Larry Ladove and he was the one who had been paid $75,000 to arrange the meeting.

The Wolf ignored Captain Ladove. "Under the circumstances, you look well," he said to Little Gus. "Very well indeed."

The Italian smiled thinly. He had a small body, but it was tight and hard. "I exercise three times a day, every day. I almost never have liquor, and not by choice. I eat well, and not by choice either."

The Wolf smiled, then said, "It sounds like

you don't expect to be here for your full sentence."

Palumbo coughed out a laugh. "That's a good bet. Three life sentences served concurrently? The discipline's in my nature, though. The future? Who can know for sure about these things?"

"Who can know? One time I escaped from a gulag on the arctic circle. I told a cop in Moscow, 'I spent time in a gulag; you think *you* can scare me?' What else do you do in here? Besides exercise and eat Healthy Choice?"

"I try to take care of my business back in New York. Sometimes I play chess with a sick madman down the hall. He used to be in the FBI."

"Kyle Craig," said the Wolf. "You think he's crazy like they say?"

"Yeah, totally. So tell me, *pakhan,* how can this alliance you suggest work? I am a man of discipline and careful planning, in spite of these humbling circumstances. From what I'm told, you're reckless. Hands-on. You involve yourself with even the smallest operations. Extortion, prostitution. *Stolen cars?* How can this work between us?"

The Wolf finally smiled, then shook his head. "I am hands-on, as you say. But I'm not reckless, not at all. It's all about the money, no? The bling-bling? Let me tell you a secret that no one else knows. This will surprise you and maybe prove my point."

The Wolf leaned forward. He whispered his secret, and the Italian's eyes suddenly widened with fear. With stunning quickness, the Wolf grabbed Little Gus's head. He twisted it powerfully, and the gangster's neck broke with a loud, clear snap.

"Maybe I am a little reckless," said the Wolf. Then he turned to the camera in the room. He spoke to Captain Ladove of the guards. "Oh, I forgot, no touching."

The next morning Augustino Palumbo was found dead in his cell. Nearly every bone in his body had been broken. In the Moscow underworld, this symbolic kind of murder was known as *zamochit*. It signified complete and total dominance by the attacker. The Wolf was boldly stating that he was now the godfather.

Part One

THE "WHITE GIRL" CASE

Chapter 1

THE PHIPPS PLAZA shopping mall in Atlanta was a showy montage of pink-granite floors, sweeping bronze-trimmed staircases, gilded Napoleonic design, lighting that sparkled like halogen spotlights. A man and a woman watched the target — "Mom" — as she left Niketown with sneakers and whatnot for her three daughters packed under one arm.

"She *is* very pretty. I see why the Wolf likes her. She reminds me of Claudia Schiffer," said the male observer. "You see the resemblance?"

"Everybody reminds you of Claudia Schiffer, Slava. Don't lose her. Don't lose your pretty little Claudia or the Wolf will have you for breakfast."

The abduction team, the Couple, was dressed expensively, and that made it easy for them to blend in at Phipps Plaza, in the Buckhead section of Atlanta. At eleven in the morning, Phipps wasn't very crowded, and that could be a problem.

It helped that their target was rushing about

in a world of her own, a tight little cocoon of mindless activity, buzzing in and out of Gucci, Caswell-Massey, Niketown, then Gapkids and Parisian (to see her personal shopper, Gina), without paying the slightest attention to who was around her in any of the stores. She worked from an At-a-Glance leather-bound diary and made her appointed rounds in a quick, efficient, practiced manner, buying faded jeans for Gwynne, a leather dop kit for Brendan, Nike diving watches for Meredith and Brigid. She even made an appointment at Carter-Barnes to get her hair done.

The target had style and also a pleasant smile for the salespeople who waited on her in the tony stores. She held doors for those coming up behind her, even men, who went out of their way to thank the attractive blonde. "Mom" was sexy in the wholesome, clean-cut way of many upscale American suburban women. And she did resemble the supermodel Claudia Schiffer. That was her undoing.

According to the job's specs, Mrs. Elizabeth Connolly was the mother of three girls; she was a graduate of Vassar, class of '87, with what she called "a degree in art history that is practically worthless in the real world — whatever that is — but invaluable to me." She'd been a reporter for the *Washington Post* and the *Atlanta Journal-Constitution* before she was married. She was thirty-seven, though she didn't look much more than thirty. She had her hair in a velvet barrette that morning, wore a short-sleeved turtleneck, a crocheted sweater, slim-fitting slacks. She was bright, religious — but sane about it — and tough when she needed to be, at least according to the specs.

Well, she would need to be tough soon.

Mrs. Elizabeth Connolly was about to be abducted.

She had been *purchased,* and she was probably the most expensive item for sale that morning at Phipps Plaza.

The price: $150,000.

Chapter 2

LIZZIE CONNOLLY felt light-headed and she wondered if her quirky blood sugar was acting up again.

She made a mental note to pick up Trudie Styler's cookbook — she kind of admired Trudie, who was cofounder of the Rainforest Foundation as well as Sting's wife. She seriously doubted she would get through this day with her head still screwed on straight, not twisted around like the poor little girl in *The Exorcist.* Linda Blair, wasn't that the actress's name? Lizzie was pretty sure it was. Oh, who cared? What difference did trivia make?

What a merry-go-round today was going to be. First, it was Gwynnie's birthday, and the party for twenty-one of her closest school buddies, eleven girls, ten boys, was scheduled for one o'clock at the house. Lizzie had rented a bouncy house, and she had already prepared lunch for the children, not to mention for their moms or nannies. Lizzie had even rented a Mister Softee ice-cream truck for three hours. But you never knew what to expect at these birthday gigs — other than laughter, tears, thrills, and spills.

After the birthday bash, Brigid had swimming lessons, and Merry had a trip to the dentist scheduled. Brendan, her husband of fourteen years, had left her a "short list" of his current needs. Of course everything was needed A.S.A.P.S. which meant *as soon as possible, sweetheart.*

After she picked up a T-shirt with rhinestones for Gwynnie at Gapkids, all she had left to buy was Brendan's replacement dop kit. Oh, yeah, and her hair appointment. *And* ten minutes with her savior at Parisian, Gina Sabellico.

She kept her cool through the final stages — *never let them see you sweat* — then she hurried to her new Mercedes 320 station wagon, which was safely tucked in a corner on the P3 level of the underground garage at Phipps. No time for her favorite rooibos tea at Teavana.

Hardly anybody was in the garage on a Monday morning, but she nearly bumped into a man with long dark hair. Lizzie smiled automatically at him, revealing perfect, recently whitened and brightened teeth, warmth, and sexiness — even when she didn't want to show it.

She wasn't really paying attention to anyone — thinking ahead to the fast-approaching birthday party — when a woman she passed suddenly grabbed her around the chest as if Lizzie were a running back for the Atlanta Falcons football team trying to pass through the "line of spinach," as her daughter Gwynne had once called it. The woman's grip was like a vise — she was strong as hell.

"What are you doing? Are you crazy?" Lizzie finally screamed her loudest, squirmed her hardest, dropped her shopping bags, heard something break. "Hey! Somebody, help! *Get off of me!*"

Then a second assailant, the BMW sweatshirt guy, grabbed her legs and held on tight, hurt her, actually, as he brought her down onto the filthy, greasy parking-lot concrete along with the woman. "Don't kick me, bitch!" he yelled in her face. "Don't you fucking dare kick me."

But Lizzie didn't stop kicking — or screaming either. "Help me. Somebody, help! Somebody, please!"

Then both of them lifted her up in the air as if she weighed next to nothing. The man mumbled something to the woman. Not English. Middle European, maybe. Lizzie had a housekeeper from Slovakia. Was there a connection?

The woman attacker gripped her around the chest with one arm and used her free hand to push aside tennis and golf stuff, hurriedly clearing a space in the back of the station wagon.

Then Lizzie was roughly shoved inside her own car. A gauzy, foul-smelling cloth was pushed hard against her nose and mouth, and held there so tightly it hurt her teeth. She tasted blood. *First blood,* she thought. *My blood.* Adrenaline surged through her body, and she began fighting back again with all her strength. Punching and kicking. She felt like a captured animal striking out for its freedom.

"Easy," the man said. "Easy-peasy-Japanesy . . . Elizabeth Connolly."

Elizabeth Connolly? They know me? How? Why? What is going on here?

"You're a very sexy mom," said the man. "I see why the Wolf likes you."

Wolf? Who's the Wolf? What was happening to her? Who did she know named Wolf?

15

Then the thick, acrid fumes from the cloth overpowered Lizzie and she went lights out. She was driven away in the back of her station wagon.

But only across the street to the Lenox Square Mall — where Lizzie Connolly was transferred into a blue Dodge van that then sped away.

Purchase complete.

Chapter 3

EARLY MONDAY MORNING, I was oblivious to the rest of the world and its problems. This was the way life was supposed to be, only it rarely seemed to turn out so well. At least not in my experience, which was limited when it came to anything that might be considered the "good life."

I was walking Jannie and Damon to the Sojourner Truth School that morning. Little Alex was merrily toddling along at my side. "Puppy," I called him.

The skies over D.C. were partly cloudy, but now and then the sun peeked through the clouds and warmed our heads and the backs of our necks. I'd already played the piano — Gershwin — for forty-five minutes. And eaten breakfast with Nana Mama. I had to be at Quantico by nine that morning for my orientation classes, but it left time for the walk to school at around seven-thirty. And that was what I'd been in search of lately, or so I believed. Time to be with my kids.

Time to read a poet I'd discovered recently, Billy Collins. First I'd read his *Nine Horses,* and now it was *Sailing Alone Around the Room.* Billy Collins made the impossible seem so effortless, and so possible.

Time to talk to Jamilla Hughes every day, often for hours at a time. And when I couldn't, to correspond by e-mail and, occasionally, by long flowing letters. She was still working homicide in San Francisco, but I felt the distance between us was shrinking. I wanted it to and hoped she did too.

Meanwhile, the kids were changing faster than I could keep up with them, especially Little Alex, who was morphing before my eyes. I needed to be around him more and now I could be. That was my deal. It was why I had joined the FBI, at least that was part of it.

Little Alex was already over thirty-five inches and thirty pounds. That morning he had on pin-striped overalls and an Orioles cap. He moved along the street as if a leeward wind were propelling him. His ever-present stuffed animal, a cow named Moo, created ballast so that he listed slightly to the left at all times.

Damon was lurching ahead to a different

drummer, a faster, more insistent beat. Man, I really loved this boy. Except for his fashion sense. That morning he was wearing long jean shorts, Uptowns, a gray T with an Alan Iverson "The Answer" jersey over it. His lean legs were sprouting peach fuzz, and it looked as if his whole body were developing from the feet up. Large feet, long legs, a youthful torso.

I was noticing everything that morning. I had time to do it.

Jannie was typically put together in a gray T with "Aero Athletics 1987" printed in bright red letters, sweatpant capris with a red stripe down each leg, and white Adidas sneakers with red stripes.

As for me, I was feeling good. Every now and again someone would still stop me and say I looked like the young Muhammad Ali. I knew how to shake off the compliment, but I liked to hear it more than I let on.

"You're awfully quiet this morning, Poppa," Jannie laced her arms around my free arm and said. "You having trouble at school? Your orientation? Do you like being an FBI agent so far?"

"I like it fine," I said. "There's a probationary period for the next two years. Orientation is good, but a lot of it is repetitive for me, especially what they call 'practicals.' Firing range, gun cleaning, exercises in apprehending criminals. That's why I get to go in late some days."

"So you're the teacher's pet already," she said, and winked.

I laughed. "I don't think the teachers are too impressed with me, or any other street cops. How're you and Damon doing so far this year? Aren't you about due for a report card or something?"

Damon shrugged. "We're acing everything. Why do you want to change the subject all the time when it's on you?"

I nodded. "You're right. Well, *my* schooling is going fine. Eighty is considered a failing grade at Quantico. I expect to ace most of my tests."

"*Most?*" Jannie arched an eyebrow and gave me one of Nana Mama's "perturbed" looks. "What's this *most* stuff? We expect you to ace *all* your tests."

"I've been out of school for a while."

"No excuses."

I fed her one of her own lines. "I'm doing the best I can, and that's all you can ask from somebody."

She smiled. "Well, all right, then, Poppa. Just as long as the best you can do puts all *As* on *your* next report."

About a block from the school I gave Jannie and Damon their hugs — so as not to embarrass them, God forbid, in front of all their cool-ass friends. They hugged me back and kissed their little brother, and then off they ran. "Ba-bye," said Little Alex, and so did Jannie and Damon, calling back to their brother, "Ba-bye, ba-bye!"

I picked up Little Alex and we headed home; then it would be off to work for soon-to-be Agent Cross of the FBI.

"Dada," said Little Alex as I carried him in my arms. That was right — *Dada*. Things were falling into place for the Cross family. After all these years, my life was finally close to being in balance. I wondered how long it would last. Hopefully at least for the rest of the day.

Chapter 4

NEW-AGENT TRAINING at the FBI Academy in Quantico, sometimes called "Club Fed," was turning out to be a challenging, arduous, and tense program. For the most part, I liked it, and I was making an effort to keep any skepticism down. But I had entered the Bureau with a reputation for catching pattern killers, and I already had the nickname Dragonslayer. So irony and skepticism might soon be a problem.

Training had begun six weeks before, on a Monday morning, with a crew-cut broad-shouldered SSA, or supervisory special agent, Dr. Kenneth Horowitz, standing in front of our class trying to tell a joke: "The three biggest lies in the world are: 'All I want is a kiss,' 'The check is in the mail,' and 'I'm with the FBI and I'm only here to help you.'" Everybody in the class laughed, maybe because the joke was so ordinary, but at least Horowitz had tried his best, and maybe that was the point.

FBI director Ron Burns had set it up so that my training period would last for only eight weeks. He'd made other allowances for me as well. The maximum age for entrance into the FBI was thirty-seven years old. I was forty-two. Burns had the age requirement waived for me and also voiced his opinion that it was discriminatory and needed to be changed. The more I saw of Ron Burns, the more I sensed that he was something of a rebel, maybe because he was an ex–Philadelphia street cop himself. He had brought me into the FBI as a GS13, the highest I could go as a street agent. I'd also been promised assignments as a consultant, which meant a better salary. Burns had wanted me in the Bureau, and he got me. He said that I could have any reasonable resources I needed to get the job done. I hadn't discussed it with him yet, but I thought I might want two detectives from the Washington PD — John Sampson and Jerome Thurman.

The only thing Burns had been quiet about was my class supervisor at Quantico, a senior agent named Gordon Nooney. Nooney ran Agent Training. He had been a profiler before that, and prior to becoming an FBI agent, had been a prison psychologist in New Hampshire. I was finding him to be a bean counter at best.

That morning, Nooney was standing there waiting when I arrived for my class in abnormal psych, an hour and fifty minutes on understanding psychopathic behavior, something I *hadn't* been able to do in nearly fifteen years with the D.C. police force.

There was gunfire in the air, probably from the nearby Marine base. "How was traffic from D.C.?" Nooney asked. I didn't miss the barb behind the question: I was permitted to go home nights, while the other agents-in-training slept at Quantico.

"No problem," I said. "Forty-five minutes in moving traffic on Ninety-five. I left plenty of extra time."

"The Bureau isn't known for breaking rules for individuals," Nooney said. Then he offered a tight, thin smile that was awfully close to a frown. "Of course, you're Alex Cross."

"I appreciate it," I said. I left it at that.

"I just hope it's worth the trouble," Nooney mumbled as he walked off in the direction of Admin. I shook my head and went into class, which was held in a tiered symposium-style room.

Dr. Horowitz's lesson this day was interesting